love from

Sue & Gertie
x   x

'In Loving Memory of
Gertie's best friend
Rosie Posie'

The Adventures Of Gertie Grizzler

GERTIE'S RUMBLING TUMMY

Written by Sue Katz
Illustrated by Margit Mulder

Gertie Grizzler's tummy was rumbling. She checked her alarm clock again, now it said 8 o'clock. Mr. Jones delivered her breakfast at the same time every morning, but today he was one hour late.

"I wonder where he can be?" thought Gertie **"I can't possibly start my day without a nice big, warm bowl of porridge. Has he forgotten that breakfast is the most important meal of the day?"** Gertie mumbled as she got up and had a big stretch.

She crawled slowly over to the entrance of her den and peeped out to see if there was any sign of Mr. Jones with her porridge. But as her paws leant on the door, slowly it began to open.

"How very strange!" thought Gertie, "Maybe I will go and see if Mr. Jones is OK."

As she wandered away from the safety of her home, Gertie did not even know where to look for Mr. Jones, or more importantly, where the kitchen was.

At the end of the long narrow path, Gertie came to a crossroad. Left or right? She did not have a clue. So doing what every bear in the world is taught to do, she lifted her nose high up into the air and had a big sniff.

"**Wow!**" gasped Gertie.
"**I have never smelt anything
that delicious – ever.**"
The smell in the air was so
strong that Gertie's nostrils
took control of her feet and
before long she had arrived at
the main gates of the zoo.

As Gertie walked through the gates, she looked back and saw a big sign that read:
Welcome To The Zoo

"Oh dear," thought Gertie **"I really think I should go back inside."** but her nose began twitching again as the wonderful smell seemed to get stronger and stronger.

As Gertie's nose led the way, her feet followed and it was not long before she arrived in the high street with her nose pressed up against the glass window of Mr. Harry's Salt Beef Restaurant.

"**Wow wee!**" thought Gertie.

Peering inside she saw a big slab of beef sitting on the edge of the counter.

"**That looks double delicious!**" Gertie exclaimed noticing that there was no one inside the shop. "**Perhaps I'll pop inside for a better look**" she thought.

There was only one problem. As Gertie got to the counter, she could not stop herself from having a little nibble of the warm meat. Then before you can say: **"salt beef and chips"**, she had guzzled up the lot.

Suddenly there was a loud **BANG!** The back door of the restaurant flew open and out popped Mr. Harry, the owner.

"Oh my gosh!" said Mr. Harry, **"You have eaten all my salt beef! That was supposed to be lunch for my customers!"**

"I'm very sorry. I was just so hungry, because Mr. Jones forgot my breakfast this morning." said Gertie.

"Not Mr. Jones from the Zoo?" enquired Mr. Harry.

"Yes, do you know him?" asked Gertie.

"Of course I know him. He's one of my best customers. In fact, you've just eaten his lunch!"

"Oh no!" moaned Gertie. "Now I'm going to be in even bigger trouble!"

The bear sank her head into her paws and started to cry.

"There, there big bear, don't you worry."
said Mr Harry. "I'm going to call Mr. Jones
and explain everything."

"Really? That would be so kind of you." Gertie
whimpered. "Can you tell him my nose
took over and I never meant to leave my home?"

"Of course I will. But first I need to cook a new piece of beef for my lunchtime customers."

"Oh!" Gertie perked up. "Do you need any help in the kitchen?"

"I think it might be safer if you stay here and wait for Mr. Jones to come and collect you." suggested Mr. Harry.

"You're probably right. I'll sit on the floor and I promise to try not to eat anything else."

Gertie didn't have to wait
long for Mr. Jones to arrive.

"Am I in big trouble?"
asked Gertie, nervously
hiding behind Mr. Harry.
**"I was so worried. You've
never been late with my
porridge before. So, I
came looking for you."**

"That was very kind of you Gertie, but you must never leave home without me."

"I understand, Mr. Jones. It will never happen again. I promise."

"**Good.**" nodded Mr. Jones, "**I am glad. Now come on Gertie, let's go back to the zoo.**"

Gertie followed Mr. Jones to the front door when Mr. Harry suddenly exclaimed: **"Hang on! You've forgotten your lunch."**

"Oh yes! And it's such a lovely day, I was thinking of having a picnic in the park." said Mr. Jones.

"Give me two minutes and I'll make your sandwich."

"Mr. Harry, is there any chance you can make that two sandwiches please? I'd like to invite a friend of mine to join me."

"No problem," said Mr. Harry, **"Two sandwiches coming right up!"**

Mr. Jones and Gertie came out of the restaurant a few minutes later. **"Which way is home?"** asked Gertie.

"Well we really should turn right but as I was late this morning with your breakfast, I was wondering if you would like to join me for a picnic lunch in the park before we go back to the zoo?"

"Oooh !" said Gertie. **"Another slice of that delicious meat? I think it would be very rude of me to say no!"**

"Come on then, follow me."
said Mr. Jones, leading the way.

Gertie and Mr. Jones sat eating their
sandwiches at the top of a steep hill.
In the distance they could see the whole
of the big city.

"I think this has been the most exciting day
I have ever had. Thank you Mr. Jones!"

"You are welcome Gertie. Here's to many
more adventures together!"

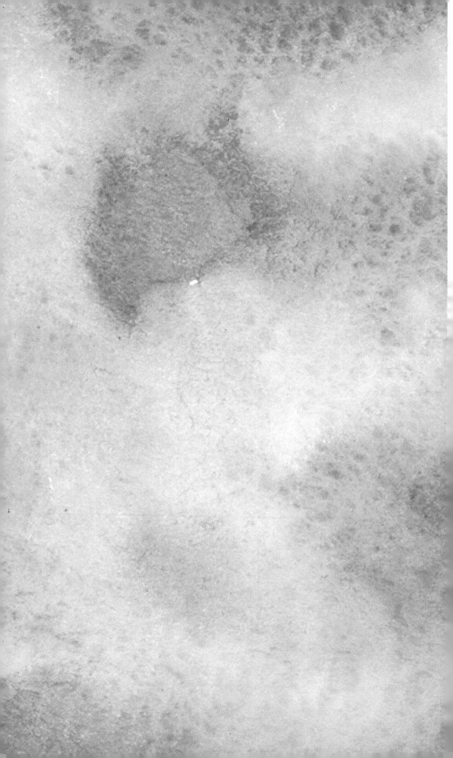